Linda's Lie

Linda's Lie

Bernard Ashley

Illustrated by Janet Duchesne

Julia MacRae Books

A division of Franklin Watts

Text © 1982 Bernard Ashley
Illustrations © 1982 Janet Duchesne
All rights reserved
First published in Great Britain 1982 by
Julia MacRae Books
A division of Franklin Watts Ltd.
12a Golden Square, London W1R 4BA
and Franklin Watts Inc.
387 Park Avenue South, New York 10016.

Reprinted 1984, 1985

British Library Cataloguing in Publication Data
   Ashley, Bernard
   Linda's lie—(Blackbirds)
   I. Title
   823'.914[J] PZ7

ISBN 0–86203–099–4 UK edition
ISBN 0–531–04576–5 US edition
Library of Congress Catalog No. 82–81792

Phototypeset by Ace Filmsetting Ltd., Frome, Somerset
Made and printed in Great Britain by Camelot Press, Southampton

Chapter 1

"What's that school playing at? Don't they know there's no pound pieces here to spare for *outings*?" Mr. Steel said the word as if it tasted bad in his mouth.

Linda looked up at his stern, black face, at the eyes which were telling a different story to the mouth. Her father smacked his knee with the flat of his hand. She knew that sign. He was just as angry with himself for not having the money to spare.

But still she said it. She wanted him to know all the facts before they threw a cover over the whole idea, like putting the yellow canary to sleep for the night. "It's the ballet," she said, "*The Sleeping Beauty* in a theatre. That's why it's a pound."

"I'll do you a dance for sixpence, girl." He smiled: but once more his

eyes and his mouth were at odds.

"The letter says see Miss if it's hardship over money . . ."

She thought his head was going to hit the ceiling. "Hardship over money? *Hardship over money*? Sweet Lord, I'll give your Miss 'hardship over money'! Does she know there's no money to go looking for work some mornings? Does she know your brother needs new shoes, your mattress can't be fit for a dog to lie

3

on, your mam and me's fed up to kingdom come with the taste of jam—and she wants to take you to the ballet! Hardship over money is right—but you don't catch me asking favours for that my girl. That don't come into it, no way!"

He pushed out of the door and thumped up the stairs to the bathroom—while the canary screeched in fright and seed went flying all over.

Linda climbed onto a chair and pulled the cover over the bird. "There!" she said. "Now shut up— 'cos that's that!" And on flat feet she went to find her mam, all that walking on her toes forgotten.

Chapter 2

Linda didn't really know how to tell Miss Smith. She knew her teacher wanted all of them to go, and she knew the school had money for the ones who couldn't afford it. Which meant Miss Smith would be upset if Linda's parents didn't want to ask for it.

"Don't you *want* to go, Linda?" she'd ask. "I always thought you were so keen." How could she tell her that her daddy didn't think it was important? That would be like saying something against Miss Smith.

The other trouble was, it was always done in the open—all in the classroom where the others could hear. Wouldn't Donna Paget make a meal of it? A fuss like that. And Jason Paris? He could squash you down with something he said as easy as he squashed other people's plasticine.

No. She'd have to find some other excuse. She was going to have to tell Miss Smith a lie.

In the classroom Monday morning all the money was starting to come in. There were pounds here and pounds there, some held out on palms like sports day medals and others clutched tight like family jewels. Even Jason Paris had his, a handful of heavy silver in tens, clunking on the table top.

Linda's name came halfway down the girls. Most times people were getting noisy by then—but today they were as quiet as mice.

"Linda Steel?"

"Please, Miss, I'm not going,
Miss." Linda felt bad already, and
she was only telling the truth so far.

Miss Smith looked up at her,
surprised. Across the other side
Donna Paget coughed, or
something.

"You're not going, Linda? Oh
dear. Why ever not?" For a second
or two she sat waiting for the
reason: then she must have guessed
it could be awkward. "Come up
here, love."

Linda went out to the front.
Everyone stared. It was still so
quiet she felt like a dancer about to
do one of the hard bits.

"Please, Miss," Linda said,

stopping and taking a deep breath, getting close enough to smell the teacher's hair. "I've got to go to a christening."

"Really? On a Monday?"

"I think it's special," she said in a low voice. She looked at Miss Smith. She was nodding.

Lying was easier than she thought. All you had to do was say it.

"Well, they can't change that, I suppose. And we can't change the day, either. What a shame—and you're one of my best dancers."

Linda smiled a brave, sad smile which said all she needed. A lie smile. That was easy, too.

"What church is that, then?" Donna Paget asked at playtime. Donna had very good ears, Linda thought—or else she could *see* what people said.

"Somewhere up London. A special one. They have their Sundays on Mondays."

"That's silly. Never heard of that before."

"Well, you have now, haven't you?"

"Who's it being christened?"

"My uncle," Linda said. She didn't know what made her say it, what made the lie get bigger. But she had heard of grown-ups having it done—and this day did have to be a bit special.

Donna Paget crossed her legs the way her mother did when she busted her sides. "They'll have a job lifting him up for the water bit," she laughed.

Linda stared her out. "He's not very heavy," she answered.

But she knew that was wrong. The whole thing was going wrong already—and she'd only just started the lie.

Chapter 3

Mr. Steel came away from the window and crackled the envelope in his fingers. He walked past the end of the out-of-work line and found a hard bench to sit on. Carefully, he opened what he had in his hand. When he hadn't earned it, it hardly seemed his to touch, let alone his to risk tearing. But he counted it, the notes and the jangle of coins which came last.

He sighed. There was a use for it all, and none left over. Shaking his head, he turned up his collar and went out. It was a long walk home when you had to pretend the buses weren't going your way.

But the buses going past weren't passing just him. With all the rest of the traffic they were skimming past a stranded car at the side of the road. The car rocked with the buffeting of air, and the man who was bent over by the wheel was swearing.

"Blessed garages!" he said, throwing the wheel-brace into the kerb. "They don't think someone might have to undo these blessed nuts!"

Mr. Steel stopped. He knew the

problem. Garages put the wheel-nuts on with special tools, and getting them off when you had a puncture was murder.

"Stupid little wheel-brace!" the man was saying. "It's got no *push*."

The man was in a suit, but his hands and face were grimy with car dirt.

Mr. Steel stopped. "Let's have a go, mate. See if a fresh pair of hands can do it."

The man looked hard at Mr. Steel and picked up the wheel-brace. "Thanks a lot," he said.

Mr. Steel took a firm grip and pulled, and pushed. But he couldn't shift any of the nuts on his own.

"Give it a go together," he said, rubbing his hands and drawing breath.

They had to hug to do it. Hands just fitting side by side on the wheel-brace, arms round each other's waists. Cheek to cheek, black and white, breathing in each other's

breath, they one-two-three'd, and strained, and arched . . . and shifted the first nut. And then the other three.

"Phew! Thanks a lot, mate. I'm very grateful to you." He pushed an oily hand into his pocket and pulled out a pound piece. "You'll have a drink with me, won't you?"

Mr. Steel looked at the man. Don't spoil it by offering me money, his eyes seemed to say. And then they seemed to think of something else.

"All right, friend, I will." He took the coin. "Good health," he said.

"Cheers," said the man. "You saw me out of trouble, there."

Chapter 4

At home, the last thing Linda wanted was any talk of ballet, or dancing, or theatres. Even school seemed a dangerous subject to get on. She didn't want her father angry about the outing, or sorry. She didn't want her mother taking her side or her brother Michael asking questions. She had started something off—something bad— and all she wanted now was for next Monday to come and go with nothing said.

She'd have liked to hibernate till Tuesday. But she couldn't do that. She had to stew inside, and act normal.

That evening she sat in front of the television in dread of *Blue Peter* doing a bit about the ballet. Or of Michael kicking his leg over the chair arm and asking whose room she'd go in when her class was out. She didn't want him looking for her in school that day.

What did you do out of school all day anyway? Someone could see you—even your father, when he was out looking for work!

Her heart turned over when he came in. It was horrible. She wasn't pleased to see him. She had to act it. Is this what being a liar's like? she thought. This nasty pain all the time, and not being able to look straight at your dad?

And he seemed all full of himself today—taller in the doorway. But he didn't say why, not to her, nor to Michael. He looked at the TV set, hummed a little something deep in his throat and went out to the kitchen.

It was bed-time before Linda
found out what it was. And then it
wasn't her father who told her. He
wasn't a showy man.

"Look!" said her mother as she
tucked Linda in on the lumpy
mattress. She held out a shiny
pound piece. "This is for your
outing. Your daddy got it extra
today. Did a little job for a man he
met. We won't miss it, being extra."
She was smiling such a happy smile.

Linda looked up at the coin. It
should have looked good and made
her smile, but it didn't. It looked like
money from another country. Even
the Queen looked cross as if she was
saying, "We've found you out,
Linda Ann Steel. Look where lying
leads you . . ."

Linda's eyes filled with tears.
She put her head under the blankets
to hide them—and she suddenly felt
like their silent canary must feel—
covered, and trapped: only she was
in a cage of lies.

"Ah—don't cry, Petal." Her
mother patted the mound of her
head. "It's a happy ending to the
story, eh?"

Chapter 5

The cold coin in Linda's sock
seemed to stick out like some nasty
bite. You could see it if you knew
where to look for it, even with white
socks on. And you'd see where it had
been when she took them off for
dance, grazing her all grey where it
scratched her ankle.

But she didn't know what else to
do with it. She couldn't just give it
in and say she was going to the
ballet after all. Not really. They
didn't cancel christenings just like

that, and she'd made it sound much too important to just have changed her mind.

There was nowhere to hide it at home where someone wouldn't come across it—and nobody's place was secret enough in school. The only other thing would be to throw it away. But she shivered at the thought. A picture in her head of her father working for it made the money much too precious for that.

It weighed her down as if it had been in pennies. Why had she had to tell Miss Smith a lie? It had seemed easy at first, but now it was getting harder and harder every minute.

With her bag held against her leg

she went into the classroom. Today she really didn't want to be at school. But if she thought things were bad there was worse to come. Life could play some terrible tricks.

"Listen, children, I've got something important to ask you. Andrew Field has lost his ballet money. He thinks he left it in his bag in the cloakroom—silly boy— but he's just been back to look, and it isn't there."

Everyone looked at Andrew Field, mouths in little O's. He put on a tragic face and stared at his *Happy Reader.* Then they looked for Jason Paris: but he was late again. He'd kick his way into the classroom in a minute—in a mood, but innocent!

"Mind you, Andrew could have dropped it somewhere else. So if anyone comes across it I'll be very grateful."

Linda remembered past fusses about missing things. A feeling of nobody being trusted would hang in the classroom till the money was found, or it was forgotten.

"Anyway, it's our hall time now, so let's get changed for it quickly and quietly."

Now Linda had to take her socks off. And just as she knew it would, the pound piece in the right one ~~Sock~~ seemed to burn like something ~~jumped out~~ from a bonfire. If anyone saw that now it would be much too late to say she'd brought her money to go after all. There'd be all sorts of questions asked, and Donna Paget would think it was Christmas. They'd have to talk to her parents to clear it up, and then all the christening lie would come out.

"Hurry up, Linda. Come on, it's not like you to be slow for dance."

But getting off a sock with money

in it was every bit as difficult as
Linda thought it would be. The
hard-edged lump kept riding up
with her leg and seemed to want to
jump itself out and onto the floor.
And trapping it between her thumb
and her sock only left that guilty
secret showing in her hand.

There was only one last chance.
She pretended the sock was too
tight and did the other one instead.
If she hid the money leg, she told
herself, she could do it while the

others went out of the room.

She pulled her dress over her head, folded it with the one sock hidden, and sat up straight with her arms on the desk. Ready. The whole room was ready.

"Good." Miss Smith stood up.

"Please, Miss, Linda Steel's left one sock on!" Donna Paget sounded as if she'd discovered a new planet. And everyone laughed as if it was the best joke ever invented. Even Andrew Field forgot he was supposed to be worried sick about his money.

Linda closed her eyes. Tight, dry, guilty eyes.

"Come on," said Miss Smith.

"Silly girl. Clocks won't stop for you." She hurried in a zig-zag between the tables. "Cock your leg up."

There was nothing else Linda could do. She was done for. Inside she had that empty, helpless feeling of just going off under gas at the dentist's. She felt Miss Smith lift her foot, and she thought she heard her own voice saying something beginning with "I . . ." She could hear the class laughing at the sight of Miss Smith helping her. But no noise was loud enough to cover the sound of the pound as its hard, ringing edge hit the floor.

"Whee, Miss . . ."

"Linda Steel!"

"Hey, look, Andrew . . ."

Public shock. Private glee. Even good friends drew in their breath.

"I think you'd better take this money and have a little talk with Mrs. Cheff, Linda," said Miss Smith. "Don't you?"

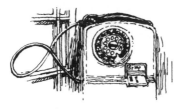

Chapter 6

It was a cold and windy morning but Mr. Steel forced himself to be up and out at his old time for work. It did no good to let things slide. Besides, there was something special he had to do before he could rest easy in his mind.

He went to the end of the street and pulled himself into the telephone box. In a few moments—using the phone as an ear-muff against the icy blast coming through a broken pane—he was talking to Linda's headmistress.

"It's a jolly good job you phoned," Mrs. Cheff told him after hearing what he wanted. "Linda's not down as going, not on the list. She said something about going to a christening."

Mr. Steel frowned. It was a bad line and the cold wind was howling. It had almost sounded like *christening*, what the headmistress had said. "No, it's the dancing she wants. I give her the money, only it was late and I was scared the seats had all run out."

"Really, they get so muddled!" Mrs. Cheff complained. "And they seem to think money grows on trees, don't they?"

Mr. Steel didn't answer. That bit didn't sound like Linda.

"I'll find out why she hasn't paid. I'm sure we've still got a seat. I just hope she hasn't lost the money."

"So do I," said Mr. Steel. "So do I." And shaking his head he put the phone back on its cold cradle.

Chapter 7

Mrs. Cheff took Linda into her room. She sat in her swivel chair and looked at the red-eyed girl. "Really, Linda! You do seem to have lost your senses. How could you be so stupid with someone else's money?"

Linda's toes curled into the flattened carpet. She frowned at Mrs. Cheff's knees. Everything had got out of hand so quickly. She didn't know what to do, what to say. If she told Mrs. Cheff the truth,

what would her father say about the
lie? But, then, what would he say
about them thinking she'd stolen
somebody's pound?

"It's just as well the pound turned
up, isn't it?"

Linda stared at Mrs. Cheff. But
she kept her mouth shut tight. How

did she know about the money down her sock? Miss Smith hadn't told her—she'd left that to Linda. Could she see through the wall or something, like she always said she could?

"Your father phoned—sensible man—so I knew you had a pound to pay. No thanks to you, Linda, was it?"

Linda shook her head. He'd phoned? Then Mrs. Cheff knew she was supposed to go. That meant she knew she wasn't a thief. But it also meant she'd found out about the lie!

"Although I still don't know why you said you were going to a christening. Your father didn't seem to understand either. Unless it was something to do with what we're going to see. *The Sleeping Beauty.* Was it some silly joke about seeing the baby's christening on the stage?"

It went very quiet in the small room. Linda heard the sounds of music from the hall and wished she were there with the rest of the class.

LITTLE GREY RABBIT'S
VALENTINE

LITTLE GREY RABBIT'S VALENTINE

By Alison Uttley
Pictures by Margaret Tempest

templar publishing

ROBIN THE POSTMAN stood in the shelter of the holly bush, staring down at a heap of letters. "It will take me hours to sort all these," he sighed. "St Valentine's Day tomorrow, and all these little messages to be delivered. I shall want help. I need an ass–ass–assistant. I can't do it. I really can't."

He turned over the tiny leafy envelopes with his beak, and flipped them with his wing and pushed them with his slender toes. Most of them were holly leaves but a few were brown beech leaves, and one was a cabbage leaf.

"Scores of Valentines, and who can be trusted to help? Not a bird can I ask, they will all be too busy billing-and-cooing, getting their love-songs ready, wetting their whistles. It's their courting day tomorrow."

Footsteps came padding along the lane, and Milkman Hedgehog came up with his milk cans. "Hello, Robin," said he, and he stopped and looked in astonishment.

"What's this? A windy day brought down all these, Robin?" he asked.

"Valentines," said Robin. "I'm snowed under with them."

"Why, it's St Valentine's Day tomorrow!" cried old Hedgehog. "I must send my missis one. Something short and sweet, like:

'Prickles is sharp and so are you
You're still my sweetheart
I love you true'."

The Robin wasn't listening.

"Milkman Hedgehog," said he suddenly. "Could you help me to deliver these Valentines tomorrow?" he asked.

"Me?" cried Hedgehog. "I can't read."

"No need. There are pictures on most of them," said Robin. "You can carry them in your milkcans. I'll sort them out and make it easy for you. Do help me," pleaded the Robin. "I'll lend you my second-best postman's hat, too. You'll be the assistant postman."

"Assistant postman? Well, well," hesitated the Hedgehog.

"Come here at dawn, when you've done milking, and I'll give you the Valentines,' said the Robin.

"And the hat," added Hedgehog. "They won't believe it unless I wear a hat."

"Yes, the hat," cried the Robin cheerfully and he began to whistle and sing.

Old Hedgehog went on his way to the cows, and then he turned home.

"I'm going to help Postman Robin tomorrow, wife," said he. "It's St Valentine's Day and he's extra busy. I'm going to wear a postman's hat," added the Hedgehog. "It makes me official, like."

Mrs Hedgehog was delighted and Fuzzypeg danced with joy.

"My father's going to be a postman," he boasted up and down the lanes and fields.

"Whatever for?" asked Water Rat who was polishing his boat.

"It's St Valentine's Day tomorrow," said Fuzzypeg.

Water Rat counted the notches on a post by the river; one, two, three, up to thirteen. "February the Fourteenth tomorrow. St Valentine's Day," said he. "I must post my Valentine tonight."

The little Hedgehog danced away to Grey Rabbit's house and tapped on the door.

"Come in Fuzzypeg," Grey Rabbit cried. "I've been baking blackberry jam puffs, and here's one for you, hot from the oven."

"My father's going to be a postman tomorrow," said Fuzzypeg, as he took a big bite of the jam puff.

"Surely not!" cried Grey Rabbit.

"Yes, he's going to be a postman and wear a hat because Postman Robin wants a sister to help him, for St Valentine's."

"A sister for St Valentine's," shouted Hare and he leapt high.

"St Valentine's," echoed Squirrel, spinning round so rapidly her tail flew out in the wind.

"I must be going," said Fuzzypeg. "Thank you, dear Grey Rabbit."

"Goodbye, Fuzzypeg," they all called, and away he went to spread his news.

"What is a Valentine, Grey Rabbit?" asked Squirrel.

"It's a picture or a message for one you love, and you mustn't put your name. It's a surprise," said Grey Rabbit.

"Then how do you know who sent it?" asked Hare.

"You try to guess," said Grey Rabbit.

"Well, I'm going to make my Valentine now," said Hare. "And me too," said Squirrel, and Grey Rabbit nodded.

They all sat down at the table with pen and ink and paint-brushes and leaves. The pens were quills from the goose, and the brushes were made of feathers which the Speckledy Hen gave them. The ink was the 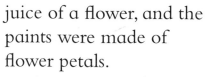 juice of a flower, and the paints were made of flower petals.

A great scratching came from Hare's pen and he stuck out his tongue as he wrote.

"Who's going to have your Valentine, Hare?" whispered Squirrel very softly so that Grey Rabbit would not hear.

"It's for the Fox," whispered Hare. "I'm doing a special Valentine for him."

"But he's not your special friend," protested Squirrel.

"I'm sending it to my special enemy," said Hare.

Squirrel stared. She licked her quill pen and waited. "How do you spell Love, Grey Rabbit?" she asked loudly.

"L-O-V-E," said Grey Rabbit.

"I thought that was for a loaf of bread," said Squirrel.

"I'm good at rhyming," boasted Hare. "Love, Dove."

He dipped his pen in the ink and he began to write. "Fox, Box, Nox, Wox," he muttered, and he made his Valentine.

> "Mister Fox.
> You'll get some Nox.
> Beware.
> From Hare."

He lighted a candle and sealed his letter with scarlet sealing-wax so that it looked like a holly berry on the holly leaf.

"You are clever, Hare," said Squirrel, enviously. "I can't do mine."

"Put your thinking-cap on," said Hare, and Squirrel tied her handkerchief in a bonnet on her head.

"It has worked," she cried. "The thinking-cap helped me. I can do it now."

She scribbled for a few minutes and then read aloud her Valentine:

> "When this you see
> Remember me,
> And drink your tea."

"It is for Moldy Warp," she explained.

Grey Rabbit was struggling with her Valentine, which was for Wise Owl because nobody else would send him one.

"Lend me your thinking-cap, Squirrel," said she. "I can't do it."

She went to her writing-desk, and at once she wrote Wise Owl's message:

"The Owl is wise,
He's full of eyes,
And when he cries
Too-whit, too-whoo,
I love him too,
I do, I do."

She had to take three holly leaves and pin them together to make her long Valentine for the Owl.

"I'll give them to the Robin," said Hare.

While the three animals were busy making their Valentines, Water Rat leapt into his boat and rowed out to the middle of the stream. There, with ducks laughing at him, he wrote on a lily-leaf, then threw it away, for all he could say was "Love, Dove."

He rowed back to the shore and hurried to his home.

"Oh, Mrs Webster, do help me to make a Valentine," he cried to his housekeeper. "It won't rhyme."

"I know nothing of rhymes," said fat Mrs Webster, "but I can make some nice Valentines, such as any young person would like to get. Just leave it to me."

Mrs Webster went back to the kitchen, where she made some St Valentine's cakes, of duck eggs and sugar and butter. She looked in her cupboard for the St Valentine's cutter, which was in the shape of a heart. She cut a dozen little yellow cakes, and dropped a dried chamomile flower on each. Then she baked them in the oven, and left them to cool.

On St Valentine's Day the birds were singing very early to one another, for every bird got up at dawn to sing to his dearest one.

"What a noise the birds are making," yawned Hare.

"It's St Valentine's Day," Grey Rabbit reminded him. "It's the birds' courting day and they sing to their sweethearts."

"Hum," grunted Hare. "Sweethearts.
I could do with a sweet heart for breakfast.
I'm hungry. I'd like a heart made of sugar
and spice."

"There's a dove calling. Listen," said
Squirrel.

"Coo-roo. Coo-roo. I love true." cooed
the dove in the tree. Hare went to the door
and looked out.

Old Hedgehog was already coming with the milk. He carried one pail of milk and one pail of letters. On his head a tiny black hat was perched.

"Good morning, everybody," said he. "I'm the assistant postman. A happy St Valentine's Day to you. Here's a Valentine for Miss Grey Rabbit, and one for Miss Squirrel and two for Mister Hare."

"Oh, thank you. Thank you, kind assistant postman," said the three, and they carried their Valentines to the table. Milkman Hedgehog filled the jug with new milk and stood for a moment on the doorstep.

"I've been very busy," he informed them. "I've got Valentines for all the rabbits, hares, hedgehogs, field mice and whatnot in the district. I don't know what's come over the animals this year. There wasn't all this Valentining when I was young. Only the birds sent Valentines, but now everybody's doing it."

"It's a nice custom," said Grey Rabbit.

"That reminds me, I've got another Valentine for you, Miss Grey Rabbit. I put it in my pocket for safety, and I nearly forgot it."

He pulled out a snow-white square envelope, addressed to Little Grey Rabbit. In the corner was a stamp, nearly as big as the letter.

"Who can have sent this?" asked Grey Rabbit, turning it over and examining it carefully. It was sealed with green wax.

"Open it and see," cried Hare, impatiently.

"Yes, open it," added Squirrel, dancing with excitement.

Slowly Grey Rabbit broke the seal and opened the white envelope. She drew out a picture of a heart, painted with tiny flowers round the edge, and "Dear Grey Rabbit" printed on it.

"Who sent it?" she asked, but Hedgehog didn't know. Robin had given it to him with the rest and he had asked no questions.

"I mustn't waste time. I've these Valentines to deliver as well as my milk. Good morning, Miss," said he.

"Good morning, Hedgehog," said Grey Rabbit. Then she ran after him and pressed a tiny bottle of violet scent into his hand.

"For you, dear Milkman," she whispered.

Squirrel and Hare were reading their leafy letters. Squirrel had a nut tied to hers, and a few words were pricked on the leaf.

"Sweet Lavender, Sweet Lavender."
A Valentine lies under her."

Squirrel darted out to the garden, and there under the lavender bush lay a leafy parcel with a white wool muff, lined with scarlet.

"I do believe my Valentine is from you, Grey Rabbit," cried Squirrel. "Nobody else knew how much I wanted a white muff for these cold February days. Thank you, dear Grey Rabbit."

Hare opened his letter and read aloud the message written in large clumsy letters on a cabbage leaf.

> "O Hare so sweet,
> Will you be mine?
> I bid you meet
> Your Valentine."

"Oh! Oh!" cried Hare leaping high so that his coat tails went out like wings. "Did you hear that?"

"'O Hare so sweet'," said Squirrel, mocking. "Are you sweet?"

"'Will you be mine?'" said Grey Rabbit slowly. "Who wants you to be theirs? Who wants to meet you, Hare?"

Hare stopped and sniffed his Valentine. They all wrinkled their noses and sniffed.

"It's not violets. I gave that to Old Hedgehog," said Grey Rabbit.

"It's not lily-of-the-valley," said Squirrel. "I put a drop of that on Mole's Valentine."

"It's – it's – it's Fox!" shuddered Hare. "I remember it. He sent me this Valentine."

"Never mind, Hare. Here's a second Valentine the postman brought you."

Grey Rabbit pointed to a green leaf which had fallen on the floor.

"Darling Hare,
The Hare we love,
Look on the chair,
Below and above."

Hare ran to the rocking-chair. On the seat
lay a little parcel and under the chair
was another. He opened them and drew
out first a cobweb waistcoat with a heart
embroidered on it, and then a scarlet
handkerchief for his pocket.

"This is from you,
Grey Rabbit," he cried.
"I know it. Oh, thank
you. It's just what I want.
What a lovely Valentine."

There was a rat-tat-tat on the door. Water Rat stood there with Mrs Webster. They carried an elegant basket made of reeds from the river.

"A basket of Valentines for Miss Grey Rabbit," said Mrs Webster, curtseying. Water Rat bowed and shook his frills.

"Come in. Come in," invited Grey Rabbit.

They entered and although they brought pools of water from their clothes, nobody minded. Grey Rabbit opened the basket and saw the dozen little golden cakes in the shape of hearts.

"I was so hungry," said Hare.

"This is a sensible Valentine. Thank you Water Rat and Mrs Webster."

Mrs Webster was peeping about, for she had never seen the little house before. Grey Rabbit popped a jar of heather honey in her pocket and gave Water Rat a lace frill for his coat.

Wise Owl's present fell down the chimney. It was a little book called "The True History of the Valentine," but it had so many hard words Hare used it as a footstool.

Fuzzypeg came with his Valentine. It was a basket of snowdrops from the woods. Speckledy Hen of course sent an egg but it had the word LUV scrawled on it by the Hen's big toe.

"Who sent your special Valentine?"
asked everybody as they looked at the white
envelope with a real stamp and a flowery
heart.

"Who sent it, Grey Rabbit?"

Grey Rabbit shook her head. She had
no idea.

"I think it was Moldy Warp," said Squirrel,
but when the Mole came, he said "No."
He brought a tiny silver locket which he
had made out of a sixpence he once found.
It was the prettiest little locket and it opened
to hold a drop of dew.

They all stood in a circle and sang the Valentine song, in thanks for all the presents and love.

"St Valentine's Day. St Valentine's Day.
The birds are courting and kissing today.
We love one another whatever you say.
We are very happy this Valentine's Day."

But who sent the Valentine? Perhaps it was a Fairy, or even St Valentine himself.
I cannot tell you for it is my secret, but perhaps it was a little boy or girl. I leave you to guess.

DEAR GREY RABBIT

WHICH LITTLE GREY RABBIT BOOKS DO YOU HAVE?

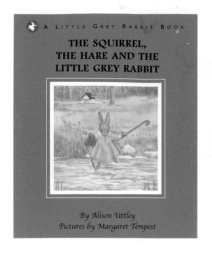

A LITTLE GREY RABBIT BOOK

THE SQUIRREL, THE HARE AND THE LITTLE GREY RABBIT

By Alison Uttley
Pictures by Margaret Tempest

A LITTLE GREY RABBIT BOOK

HOW LITTLE GREY RABBIT GOT BACK HER TAIL

By Alison Uttley
Pictures by Margaret Tempest

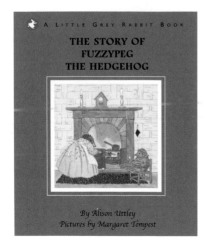

A LITTLE GREY RABBIT BOOK

THE STORY OF FUZZYPEG THE HEDGEHOG

By Alison Uttley
Pictures by Margaret Tempest

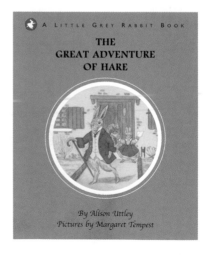

A LITTLE GREY RABBIT BOOK

THE GREAT ADVENTURE OF HARE

By Alison Uttley
Pictures by Margaret Tempest

SQUIRREL GOES SKATING

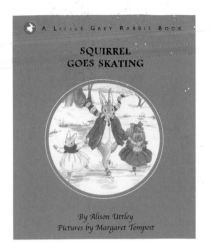

By Alison Uttley
Pictures by Margaret Tempest

LITTLE GREY RABBIT'S CHRISTMAS

LITTLE GREY RABBIT'S VALENTINE

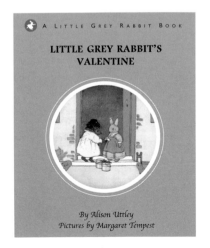

By Alison Uttley
Pictures by Margaret Tempest

HARE AND THE EASTER EGGS

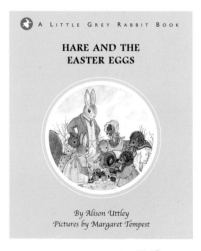

By Alison Uttley
Pictures by Margaret Tempest

A TEMPLAR BOOK

This edition first published in the UK in 2015 by Templar Publishing,
an imprint of The Templar Company Limited,
Deepdene Lodge, Deepdene Avenue, Dorking, Surrey, RH5 4AT, UK
www.templarco.co.uk

Original edition first published in the UK in 1953
by William Collins Sons & Co Ltd

This edition edited by *Susan Dickinson* and *Katie Haworth*
Additional design by *janie louise hunt*

1 3 5 7 9 10 8 6 4 2

ISBN 978-1-7837-0-195-7

Printed in China